School Lunch

TRUE KELLEY

Holiday House / New York

Library of Congress Cataloging-in-Publication Data
Kelley, True.
School lunch / by True Kelley.— 1st ed.
p. cm.
Summary: When Harriet, the cook at Lincoln School,
goes on a much-needed vacation, the staff and students
send her letters complaining about her replacements and
trying to persuade her to return.
ISBN 0-8234-1894-4 (hardcover)
[1. Schools—Fiction. 2. Food—Fiction. 3. Cooks—Fiction.
4. Letters—Fiction.] I. Title.

PZ7.K2824Sc 2005
[E]—dc22
2004054152
ISBN-13: 978-0-8234-1894-7
ISBN-10: 0-8234-1894-4

Hooray for Carol Piroso,
Simonds School Lunchroom Lady

Harriet, the cook, was tired. It was hard work cooking good, healthy lunches for the kids at Lincoln School. Mrs. Hazen's class didn't like fruit. Mrs. Jones's class didn't like vegetables of any kind. Mr. Kennedy's class didn't like desserts! Harriet tried very hard to please them all. Now she needed a vacation bad!

Harriet went away to a tropical island to rest.

Mr. Fitz, the school principal, hired a substitute cook named Al. Al used to work at the diner downtown.

A week later, on the tropical island, Harriet got
her first letter from the kids telling all about him:

Dear Harriet,
    Our new cook is Al. (See enclosed photo). He has nice tattoos. He only knows how to cook bacon and eggs, greasy hamburgers, and very salty french fries. We like his food. It's different from the healthy stuff you used to give us. We miss you.
    Come back when you can.
        Love,
        Mr. Kennedy's class
P.S. The school is running out of Ketchup!

Harriet sent this postcard:

Greetings from PARADISE!

One week later Harriet got this letter and a drawing:

Dear Harriet, We are really sick of Al's food. The whole school smells like burned grease! If you smell that all morning, you aren't hungry a bit by lunchtime. You feel like you already ate. Josh found a half-dead fly in his burger. Half-dead is worse than dead. So Mr. Fitz fired Al. Al didn't seem to care. We **MISS** you. Come home soon.

Love, Mrs. Jones's class

P.S. Our new substitute cook starts tomorrow. His name is Philippe.

MY LUNCH by Josh

Harriet sent them this postcard:

Island Specialty Flaming Watermelon Compote! Super delicious! YUM! YUM!

Then Harriet got this letter:

Dear Harriet,

Philippe is a fantastic cook — especially his flaming desserts. Mr. Fitz says we are real lucky to have him due to the unfortunate fire at Chez Pierre's restaurant where he used to work. Philippe made flaming crepes yesterday and set off the school sprinkler system. (See enclosed school paper clipping.) Today we had pheasant, filet mignon, and cream tarts and baked Alaska and bon bons. The only thing we don't like is the fried frogs' legs. (Have you read The Wind in the Willows or seen Kermit the Frog?) Have a nice vacation! Love, Mrs. Hazen's class

My Crepes eez Roo-eend!

LINCOLN SCHOOL PAPER

SCHOOL SPRINKLER SYSTEM WORKS!

On Monday, Monsieur Philippe, the new school chef, made his specialty, Flaming Crêpes, in hopes of impressing all the students and teachers at the Lin̶ School. Mr. Fitz, t̶ school principal s̶ that the end resul̶ was that the scho̶ sprinkler system wa̶ successfully tested. B̶ Philip̶

Harriet sent back this postcard:

Giant Tropical Yelling Frog

HEY!!

Three weeks later she got this letter from the principal himself:

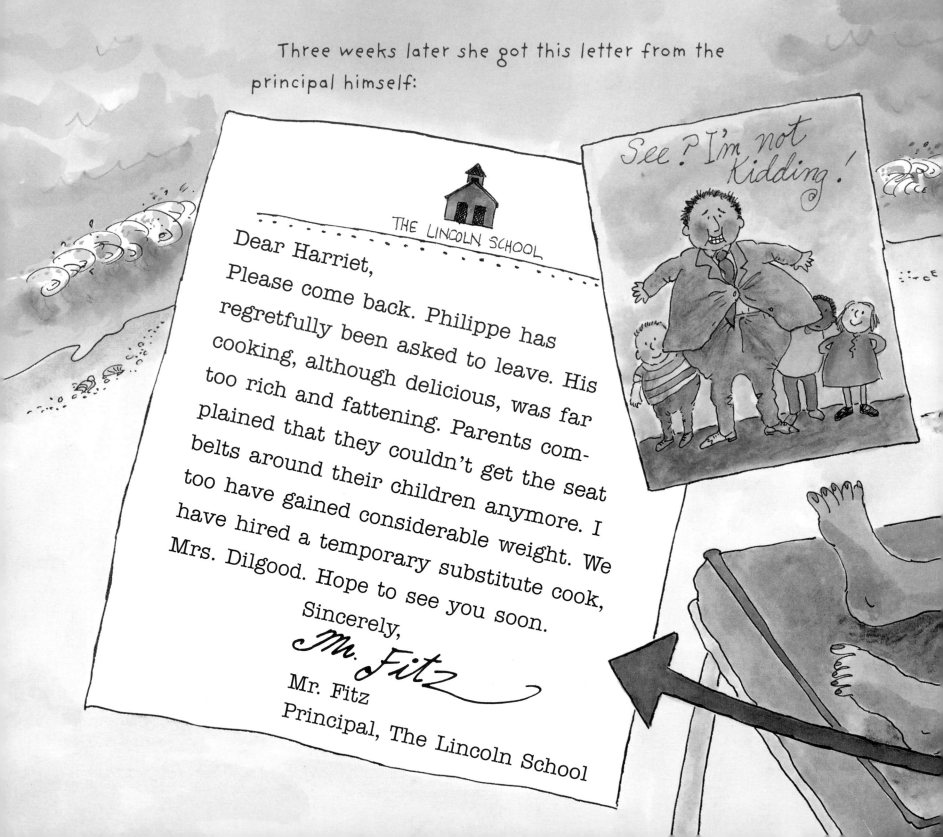

See? I'm not Kidding!

THE LINCOLN SCHOOL

Dear Harriet,
Please come back. Philippe has regretfully been asked to leave. His cooking, although delicious, was far too rich and fattening. Parents complained that they couldn't get the seat belts around their children anymore. I too have gained considerable weight. We have hired a temporary substitute cook, Mrs. Dilgood. Hope to see you soon.
Sincerely,
Mr. Fitz
Mr. Fitz
Principal, The Lincoln School

Harriet used the letter as a coaster for her pineapple strawberry tropical island fruit juice.

Soon she got another letter:

Dear Harriet,
Our new substitute cook is Mrs. Dilgood. She has cooked for years at a summer camp. She makes stuff like "Bug Juice," which might really be green Kool-Aid, and hot dogs and toasted marshmallows. It's FUN! But she just got a job cooking for the animals at the shelter, so she's leaving tomorrow! WHO will Mr. Fitz hire next? We hope you come back SOON.   Love, Mr. Keene's class
P.S. Do you know how to make S'mores?

An e-mail arrived from Mr. Fitz:

A letter arrived soon after:

by Joan

by Eliza

MR. BROWN'S CLASS

DEAR HARRIET,
OUR NEW SUBSTITUTE COOK'S NAME WAS SYBIL. (SEE ENCLOSED PICTURES.)
SHE SEEMED TO BE A ꙅꙅꙅꙅꙅꙅꙅ.
SHE LASTED ONE DAY.

BUT WHAT A DAY!

SHE MADE SOUP THAT HAD SOME VERY STRANGE INGREDIENTS. MOSTLY WE WERE GROSSED OUT, BUT GEORGE AND STEVE THOUGHT IT WAS AWESOME.
THE SALAD SORT OF CREPT OUT OF ITS BOWL AND TWINED ITSELF AROUND THINGS ... OR PEOPLE. THE DESSERT WAS CUPCAKES THAT WOULD BITE BACK IF YOU TRIED TO EAT THEM.

NO JOKE! THERE WAS
SLIMY PURPLE SLUG PUDDING, TOO.
IT SMELLED LIKE DIRTY SOCKS.

OVER ➲

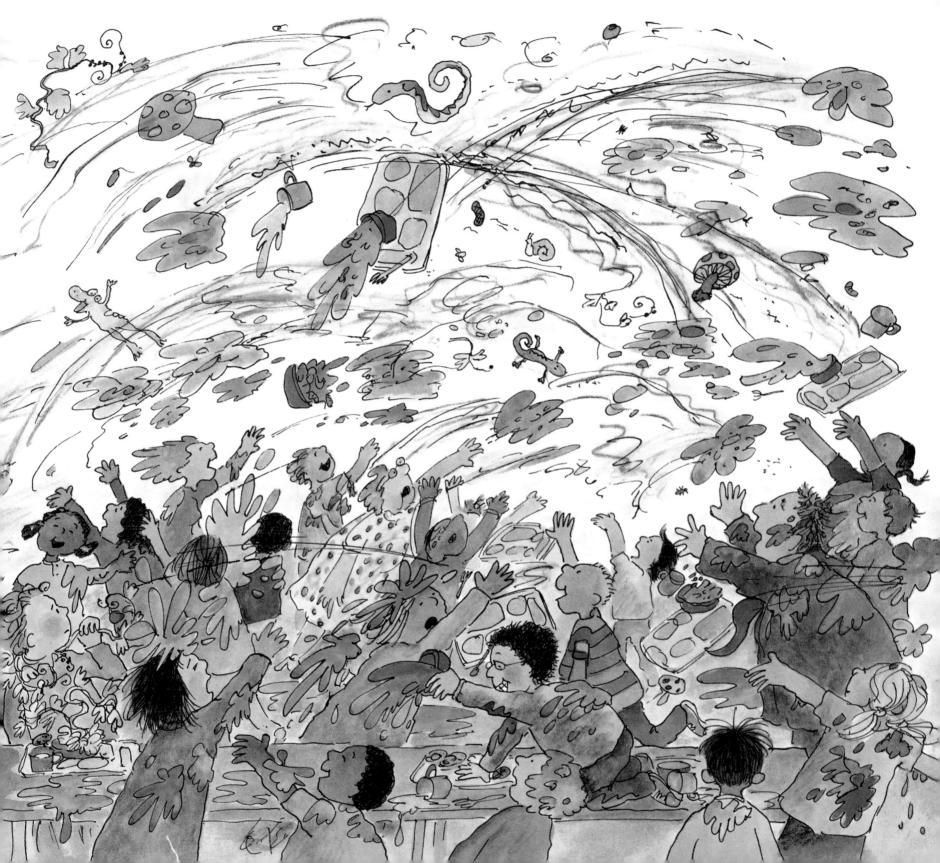

Harriet thought about that letter the whole time she ate her steaming lobster with fresh island vegetables.

Then she took a nap in a hammock.

PAGE 1

Dear Harriet,
Last week Mr. Fitz couldn't find a cook so he started using volunteers. He even had to cook for us himself. His menu sounded okay: Deep-Ocean Fish in Cream Sauce and Lime Jell-o. But he burned the whole vat of tuna casserole and the Jell-o was all green and runny.
(continued)

PAGE 2

The music teacher, Mr. Mann, ran the kitchen for a day and we had foods that made nice sounds like celery and Rice Krunchies. Nice for the ears but not really for the stomach. (continued)

Mrs. Graves, the art teacher, volunteered to cook for a day and made some pretty food that didn't taste that good.

(continued)

Yesterday was the worst because the principal's mother came in and served everyone piles of creamed spinach and lumpy yellow squash. The only one who cleaned his plate was Mr. Fitz.

(continued)

5

We are losing miss you!!! We really weight. (Are you coming back?) please COME BACK!!! Love, Mrs. Harris's class

SOON!

Harriet got this telegram from Mr. Fitz:

URGENT **=TELEGRAM=** **IMPORTANT**

KIDS NOT HEALTHY STOP

PLEASE COME BACK

EXCLAMATION POINT STOP

Harriet sat up straight in her hammock and dropped her grapes.

"Not HEALTHY!" she said. "We can't have THAT!"

The telegram slipped from her hands, dropped into the swimming pool, and sank to the bottom.

The next day in the school
lunchroom the kids were sitting at
their tables. They were quiet. Much
too quiet for a school lunchroom. They
were studying the food that sat on
their trays. No one was eating.

Mr. Fitz couldn't find a substitute cook so he had to phone in an order to the Chinese takeout restaurant. He had asked them to "cook something for the kids." The Chinese lady who took the order was new to America and didn't understand English too well yet. She thought the principal said, "Cook something for the kittens," and she had prepared some fish heads on beds of Kat Chow.

Suddenly, in through the
swinging lunchroom doors
sprang Harriet!

"HOORAY!" shouted all the kids.
"HOORAY! **HOORAY!**
HOORAY! HOORAY!!"

And from that school lunch on,
they all ate healthy foods for the rest
of their long and happy lives.